The Sound of DAY, The Sound of NIGHT

MARY O'NEILL · PICTURES BY CYNTHIA JABAR

MELANIE KROUPA BOOKS
FARRAR, STRAUS AND GIROUX   NEW YORK

The journey was difficult, but what a view!
Thank you, Mum and Dad, Deborrah, Liza, Fiona, James,
Elizabeth, Enrica, Sean, Anna, Onotse, Osho, Robert, Paul,
Lili, Richard, Jim, Sarah, Sree, Janet, and Melanie,
for inspiring me to persevere
—C.J.

Text copyright © 1966 by Mary O'Neill. © renewed 1994 by Erin Baroni and Abigail Hagler.
Illustrations copyright © 2003 by Cynthia Jabar
All rights reserved
Distributed in Canada by Douglas & McIntyre Ltd.
Color separations by Chroma Graphics PTE Ltd.
Printed and bound in the United States of America by Phoenix Color Corporation
Designed by Jennifer Browne
First edition, 2003
1 3 5 7 9 10 8 6 4 2

Library of Congress Cataloging-in-Publication Data
O'Neill, Mary Le Duc, 1905–1990
    [Sound of day]
    The sound of day ; The sound of night / by Mary O'Neill ; pictures by Cynthia Jabar.
        p.   cm.
    Summary: Two poems present the sounds of day and the sounds of night, from a clatter
of soapsuds and spatter to the hush of snowflakes touching on the ground.
    ISBN 0-374-37135-0
    1. Children's poetry, American.   2. Sound—Juvenile poetry.   3. Night—Juvenile poetry.
4. Day—Juvenile poetry.   [1. American poetry.   2. Sound—Poetry.   3. Night—Poetry.
4. Day—Poetry.]   I. Title: Sound of day ; Sound of night.   II. Jabar, Cynthia, ill.
III. O'Neill, Mary Le Duc, 1905–1990 Sound of night.   IV. Title: Sound of night.   V. Title.

PS3565.N524 S68 2003
811'.54—dc21   2002074249

The Sound of
DAY

Day sound
Is a clatter
Of soapsuds
And spatter,

Bus honks and bells,
Dishes and shoes,
Whirring of tires and
Crackle of news,

Scratch of pencils,
Scrawl of pens,

Crowing of roosters,
Cackle of hens,

Tooting of tugs,
Clicking of skates,
Opening and closing and
Latching of gates,

Twitter of birds,
Squealing of brakes,
Beating the frosting
For devil's food cakes.

Day sound is a muddle
Of talking and yelling,
Turning of pages and
Uttering spelling,

Ringing of telephones
Whistles and knocks
Fire engines screaming
Ticking of clocks

Questioning,
answering,

Licking and chewing,
Scolding and praising,

Retreating, pursuing,

Whispers and secrets,
Soft sounds and shrill—

A day simply doesn't
Know how to be still.

The Sound of
NIGHT

Small is the sound of night,
And far away
From all the lively noisings
Of the day—

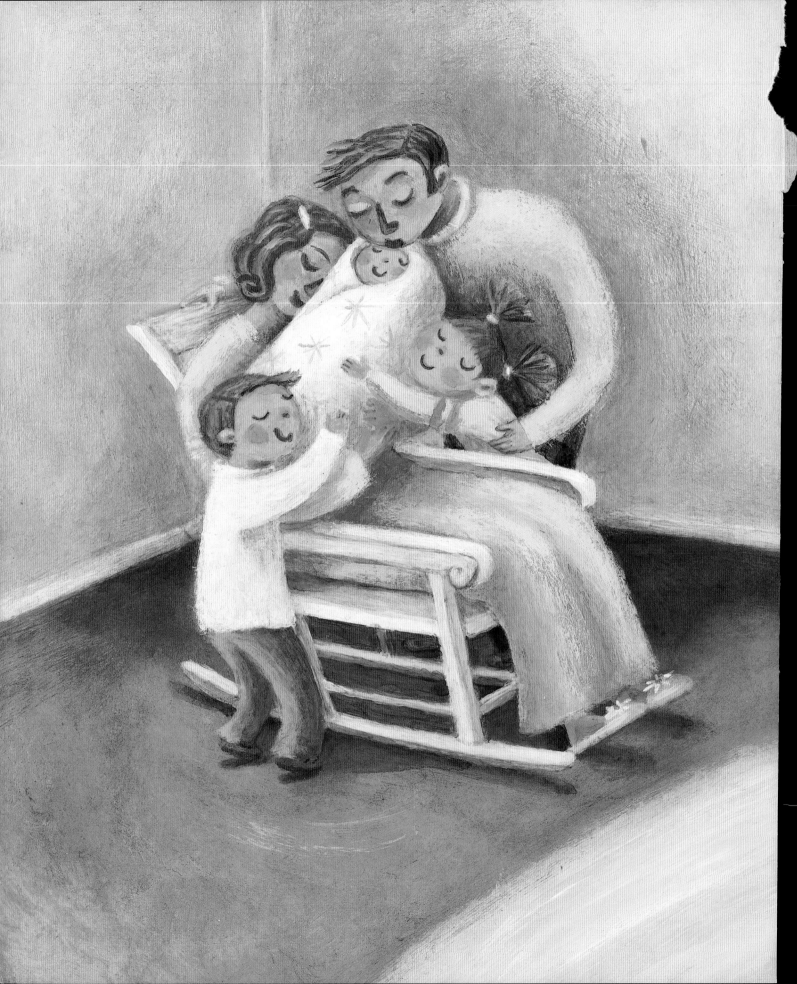

Tiptoe footsteps,
Car on road,
The tiny hopscotch
Of a toad,

Lullaby,
Airplanes whispering
In the sky,

And steadily
Upon his beat

A watchman's solid-sounding
Feet.

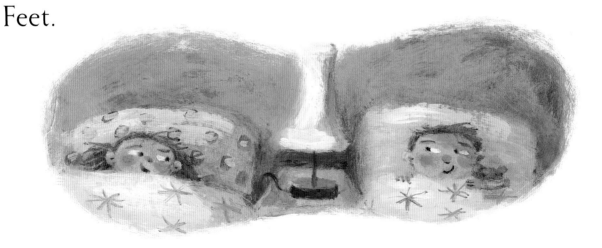

Cricket's chirp,
Family snores,
Squeakings in the
Walls and doors,

Curtain flutter,
Insect whir,
Distant dog bark,
Kitten purr,

Wind singing,
Sometimes rain
Slapping leaves on
Windowpane,

Sometimes frost's
Snap and crack
Upon the earth's old
Bony back.

And in the winter
Time of year
Comes a silence
You can hear,

As the snow
Sifts on for hours,
Filling hollows,
Frilling towers,

Muffling footsteps,
Feathering air
Until there's stillness
Everywhere—

Then the hush becomes
The sound
Of snowflakes touching
On the ground.